Follow Mr. Stink's other adventures in:

The Stink Files, Dossier 001:
The Postman Always Brings Mice

The Stink Files, Dossier 002:
To Scratch a Thief

Dossier 003:
YOU ONLY HAVE
NINE LIVES

A Novel by **Holm & Hamel**

Illustrated by Brad Weinman

HarperCollinsPublishers

The Stink Files, Dossier 003: You Only Have Nine Lives

Text copyright © 2005 by Jennifer L. Holm and Jonathan Hamel

Illustrations copyright © 2004 by Brad Weinman

All rights reserved. No part of this book may be used or reproduced in any manner whatsoever without written permission except in the case of brief quotations embodied in critical articles and reviews. Printed in the United States of America. For information address HarperCollins Children's Books, a division of HarperCollins Publishers, 1350 Avenue of the Americas, New York, NY 10019.

www.harperchildrens.com

Library of Congress Cataloging-in-Publication Data

Holm & Hamel.

You only have nine lives : a novel / by Holm & Hamel ; illustrated by Brad Weinman.— 1st ed.

p.   cm. — (The Stink files ; dossier 003)

Summary: As the new spokescat for Le Chat Gourmet cat food, former British feline spy Mr. Stink and his humans travel to France, where he revisits his childhood home and uncovers secrets about his past.

ISBN 0-06-052985-7 — ISBN 0-06-052986-5 (lib. bdg.)

[1. Cats—Fiction. 2. Spies—Fiction. 3. Twins—Fiction. 4. France—Fiction. 5. Mystery and detective stories.] I. Weinman, Brad, ill. II. Title.

PZ7.H73245Yo 2005   2004018561

[Fic]—dc22   CIP

                                                                                  AC

Typography by Karin Paprocki

1   2   3   4   5   6   7   8   9   10

❖

First Edition

For Agent W.A.H.—

thanks for keeping me on my paws.

—James

Dossier Contents

Dossier 003:
YOU ONLY HAVE
NINE LIVES

THE WATER was up to my chin. It was icy cold, and I knew I wouldn't last long, even if I could keep my head above it. To make matters worse, the level was steadily rising. Within moments, I was unable to touch the bottom with my feet. I began to paddle frantically with my paws, but the cold had worked its way into my muscles, and I was tiring fast. Every few seconds, my nose ducked beneath the water, and I came up sputtering. In short, I was drowning like a rat.

"Enjoying your swim?" a voice called mockingly.

I looked up to see a cat grinning down over the edge of the deep shaft where he had trapped me. The stone walls were slick with moss, and there was no way to climb up. Sir Archibald had always advised his operatives to swim with the tide, but this was taking it a bit far, I thought.

"The water's lovely," I said, gasping for breath. "Why don't you come down and join me?"

"Oh, I don't think so," he cackled. "I'd prefer to watch you drown."

Water rushed into my mouth and I choked.

And to think I was supposed to be on holiday!

1

Bon Voyage

T WAS a beautiful summer day in Woodland Park, New Jersey.

Mr. Green was balanced precariously on a ladder outside the pet food store, hanging a banner.

"Is it straight?" he asked his son, Aaron.

"I guess so," my boy said.

Mr. Green climbed down and admired the sign. There was a huge photo of me on it. A rather dashing photo, I might add. I smiled up at the sign too, imagining a whole new life as a famous spokescat.

PARKSIDE PET FOODS

HOME OF MR. STINK: LE CHAT GOURMET!

But no, my past life in the spy game would always haunt me. Sir Archibald and I had made too many enemies, and the diabolical Macavity was only one of them. Attracting so much attention would be hazardous to my health. The sign would have to go when we returned.

"Pretty exciting, huh, Aaron?" Mr. Green grinned. "By this time tomorrow, we'll be in Paris, the City of Light."

Aaron shrugged. "Space Camp would've been cooler. Or Disney World."

I had to disagree with my boy. Paris is the most exciting and beautiful city in the world, and I had spent quite a lot of time there, ferreting out assorted nefarious characters. There was a time when Paris had quite a reputation as a hothouse for criminals. Of course, it also had a reputation as home to some of the loveliest pussycats in the world. I, for one, was planning to look up a few old acquaintances.

"C'mon, it's gonna be great," Mr. Green enthused. "And we have Mr. Stink to thank for it all!"

What he meant was that he had entered me into a contest for Le Chat Gourmet, a delicious gourmet cat food from France. They were looking for a new spokescat—someone with culture, breeding, and impeccable taste. Not surprisingly, I had won. I am, after all, an unusually handsome Bengal cat, and in exceptional shape thanks to my counterspy experience.

Check it out. Yer famous, boss! a voice squeaked.

Can we get a raise now? another voice chimed in.

It was Frankie and Vinnie, two street mice whom I regularly used as informants.

"I'll need you two to watch the store while I'm in France," I told them.

"Sure, boss," Vinnie said. "Don'tcha worry 'bout nuttin'."

"I ain't never been nowhere but Woodland Park," Frankie said longingly, rubbing the nub of his missing tail.

"Ain't never been *nowheres,*" Vinnie corrected, smacking his partner on the shoulder. "And sure ya have. We been to Staten Island dat one time, remember?"

"Oh yeh," Frankie said, licking his lips. "Boy, dat was some *gooood* bologna."

"If you two would pay attention," I said, "there is an open bag of gerbil food in the back storeroom that you are welcome to." I stared hard at them both. "There had better be nothing else missing when I return."

"Cheese," Vinnie swore. "We don't get no respect around here."

Mr. Green was fiddling with the lock on the front door. The piranhas in the aquarium in the window looked on in dismay. Mr. Green had recently reorganized the store, and the piranhas attracted quite a bit of traffic in their new location.

"I wish Robby could come," Aaron said.

"You'll see him in two weeks." Mr. Green sighed.

"Yeah, two boring weeks," my boy groused.

"Come on now. You'll get to see castles and armor and all kinds of neat old stuff," Mr. Green said. "Let's get moving before your mother sends out the police to find us." He tapped on the window directly above a sign that read "Don't tap on the window!" "Bye, fish! Don't worry, someone will be by to feed you."

I swear one of the piranhas glared at me.

The three of us went around back to the parking lot, where we climbed into a tomato-red MGB. Mr. Green revved the engine, and I looked out happily.

Good-bye, Woodland Park, New Jersey. Bonjour, Paris!

Back at #9 North Tenth Avenue, everything was chaos.

Mrs. Green was running around looking for pass-

ports. Lily, Aaron's six-year-old sister, had a little orange suitcase of her very own and was filling it with biscuits for the trip. Or cookies, as Americans call them.

"No, Lily!" Mrs. Green said. "Put those cookies back right now."

"But what if they don't have cookies in France?" she whined.

"I'm sure they have cookies," Mrs. Green said in exasperation. "I think they invented cookies."

"I thought they invented French toast."

"Hey, hon," Mr. Green shouted. "Look what I got for Mr. Stink when we get back." He held up a box labeled "Inflatable Kiddie Pool."

"How come Mr. Stink gets his own pool?" Lily asked.

"But cats hate water," Aaron said.

"Not Bengal cats, apparently," Mr. Green said. He tossed his son a book. "Page twelve in *All About Your Bengal*."

"Really?" Aaron grabbed up the book. "Cool! Thanks!"

It is true that I enjoy the occasional swim, just for the exercise. Bengal cats like myself are famous for their love of water, unlike other breeds who fear the stuff. Some have claimed it is because the wild Asian Leopard Cat, our ancestor, hunts for food in water. But to me, it has always been proof of our proper breeding and nobility.

"Get a move on it," Mrs. Green shouted. "Or we'll miss the plane."

I had preparations of my own to make. I needed to give explicit instructions to my assistant, Kitty, on how to secure the Greens' property. I had enemies.

My previous human, Sir Archibald, had been the Director of a top-secret counterspy organization we shall call MI9. He had been murdered with a poisoned biscuit, and I had recently learned that the culprit was a six-toed fluffy white Persian cat named Macavity.

The Persian was obsessed with revenge on both Sir Archibald and myself for putting away his late human, a dealer in stolen nuclear arms. As a result of this, I was now required to take extraordinary precautions to protect my new humans.

Kitty was waiting for me by the cat door at the back. A common street cat, she was painfully skinny and had a rough kind of charm.

"Now Kitty," I said, "be on the lookout for any suspicious animals. If you see anything, especially a white Persian cat, tell Bruno immediately. Do not—and this is important, Kitty—*do not* engage the Persian directly. Do not even speak to him. He is very dangerous."

"I wish I was going," she said glumly. "I bet the mice taste different over there."

"Cats of breeding don't eat mice, Kitty," I said, exasperated.

Mrs. Green poked her head out the back door.

"Aww, how cute," Mrs. Green said, smiling at Kitty. "Mr. Stink has a girlfriend!"

Kitty blushed.

Sometimes I wish it were possible to turn off the Bristlefur charm.

Then there was no time to talk as Mrs. Green was

shouting for everyone to get into the purple minivan. As we drove down the street, we passed Bruno's house. The dog liked to trade jokes.

Hey, Bruno! I meowed to him. *What kind of dog does Dracula have?*

I don't know, Bruno barked back.

A bloodhound!

Good one, Stink! Stay away from those French poodles! They're meaner than they look.

When we reached the airport, we got into a massive line. It was with great trepidation that I sat in my cargo carrier. The last time I had traveled by air, I wound up drugged and half a planet away from my destination. Finally we reached the counter, and Mr. Green handed the tickets to the attendant.

"Any luggage?"

"We have four bags," Mr. Green said. "And one very famous cat. Ever heard of Le Chat Gourmet?"

Her expression didn't change. "Nope."

"It's gourmet cat food. Our cat's the new spokescat!"

"That's great," the attendant said. "Cat got papers?"

"Right here," Mr. Green said.

The attendant read them and smirked. "Mr. Stink? I don't smell anything."

I groaned. These humans.

"Everything's in order," the attendant said. "I'll take the cat now."

"But I thought Mr. Stink could ride on the plane with us," Aaron said, alarmed.

"He's too big to fit under the seat in front of you," the attendant replied firmly. "He goes in cargo."

I meowed loudly. What about the first-class accommodations? What about the pâté and caviar and in-flight movie?

"It'll be okay, Aaron," Mr. Green said, patting his son on the shoulder. "After all, Mr. Stink's an international traveler already, aren't you, Mr. Stink?"

My boy gave my head a last rough pat through the opening of the cat carrier. "See you in Paris, Mr. Stink," my boy said.

I remembered my last transatlantic flight and shuddered. I hoped I wouldn't wind up in Peoria.

2

My Fifteen Minutes of Fame

I **WAS DREAMING** of crème fraiche and caviar, served on elegant silver dishes, garnished with the choicest pâté of liver and tuna. Then I blinked open my eyes. It was still there! This was no dream. I looked around.

I was on a white velvet cat bed in an elegant hotel room. "Check it out, Mr. Stink!" Aaron said. He jumped onto the bed beside me, jostling me roughly.

Oh, my aching head! The cargo compartment had been hot and stuffy and filled with a team of high-strung circus Terriers, who had spent the entire seven-hour flight yipping at the top of their lungs in Chinese.

"All compliments of Le Chat Gourmet, can you believe it?" his father enthused, digging through a large gift basket overflowing with cat toys and treats.

"This hotel is something else," Mrs. Green said, sweeping open the curtains to reveal a dazzling view of Notre Dame cathedral. "I can't wait to try that Jacuzzi."

There was a knock at the door. Lily ran to fling it open. "I'm hungry! Why does Mr. Stink get all the food?"

Aaron dipped a finger into my caviar and wiggled it at his sister. "You know what caviar is, Lily? It's fish eggs!"

"Eeeeew!" she squealed.

"Ah, but only the *best* fish eggs for our most important *chat*," said a smartly dressed woman in the doorway. She was holding a clipboard.

The woman entered the room briskly and looked at me. "Well, I hope Monsieur is feeling well rested? You are even more handsome than your photograph."

I wanted to say that I was hardly looking my best after my transatlantic journey, but I meowed modestly in thanks.

"So clever, too! Who would have expected such good breeding in an American cat?" she cooed.

I was not, strictly speaking, an American cat, nor

even a British one. Sir Archibald had adopted me as a young kitten from an exclusive cat breeder's farm in the mountains right here in France.

The woman turned to the family. "My name is Veronique, and I am Monsieur Stink's publicist. We have a very busy schedule. The press conference is this afternoon."

Mrs. Green was aghast. "A press conference? For a cat?"

"*Mais oui*. Le Chat Gourmet has not had a new spokescat in over fifteen years."

"What happened to the last one?" Aaron asked.

"Ah, Renoir. It is very tragic. He choked on a hairball." She shook her head. "Now, I must see you downstairs in two hours, yes? Do not be late." She turned sharply on her heel and was gone.

As we had some time before the press conference and the Greens were hungry, I allowed them to take me down to the street in search of a café. Moments later, we were ensconced around a tiny table, I on my boy's lap. Mr. Green, whose French was noticeably rusty, ordered for everyone.

"These aren't like the French fries we get back home," Lily whined as a plate was placed in front of her.

"Oh come *on*, Lily, can't you just eat something

without complaining for once?" Aaron groaned.

Sometimes I couldn't help but be envious when I watched Aaron bicker with his sister. They might fight all the time, but she was still his sister. I had no family.

A waiter was setting a plate in front of Aaron that smelled strongly of garlic.

"What are these?" Aaron asked, poking at the little brown chunks floating in the sauce.

"Those are *escargots*," Mr. Green said. "Snails."

"You ordered snails? *Cool*," Aaron said. "Look, Lily, I'm eating snails." He waved his plate at her.

"*Mom!* Aaron's trying to make me barf!" Lily said.

"Oh, try one," Mr. Green said, picking up a tiny fork. "They're considered a delicacy here." He popped one into his mouth with gusto, and green sauce dripped down into his beard.

"And for your *chat*," the waiter said. "A dish of fresh cream, with the chef's compliments." A faint dusting of nutmeg colored the rim of the dish.

Ah, the good life, I thought as I tucked into my lunch.

French street cafés were excellent for cat watching. A pair of lovely young kittens walked by, no doubt on their way to school. A skinny street cat was filching a fish that had fallen under another table. He saw me watching him and dropped the fish.

"Oh, excuse me, Your Highness," he said, flustered. "I did not realize you were in town. Of course, this fish is yours if you wish." He bowed quickly and ran off into the alley before I could ask him what he meant.

Apparently being the spokescat for Le Chat Gourmet was a bigger deal in France than I thought.

The next two days passed in a blur.

There was a press conference where I was paraded out and photographed at every angle, and then a series of appearances at local pet food stores. My last duty was a photo shoot. Veronique briefed us on the photographer in the limousine.

"Monsieur Bertrand is magnificent! He has worked with all the best cats," she said.

When we arrived, I was promptly whisked away to hair and makeup, where a nice young Frenchman teased and styled and fluffed my fur.

"Did you just put hair spray on Mr. Stink?" Aaron asked in horror.

"But of course." The hairstylist held a mirror aloft, turning it this way and that. "There, I think we are ready now."

From what I gathered, I was to be surrounded by a

bevy of beautiful young feline models even more perfectly groomed than I. One of them in particular caught my eye. A blond-furred one with startling blue eyes. I must admit, I had a weakness for beauty.

"The name is Bristlefur, James Edward Bristlefur," I purred. "But my friends call me James."

"Anya Lapp," she said. She was Finnish. And perfectly adorable.

A short bald man wearing all black strode out onto the set.

"That's the photographer," she whispered. "Monsieur Bertrand. He is very difficult."

Monsieur Bertrand clapped his hands. "Time to begin. Places, everyone."

We were ushered onto a set that was dressed to look like a tropical rain forest. A bag of Le Chat Gourmet sat in the middle.

I heard Aaron ask, "What happens now?"

"Do not speak," Veronique snapped. "Monsieur Bertrand must concentrate."

"It is all right," Monsieur Bertrand said. "The boy is curious." He ruffled Aaron's hair, and my boy made a face. "The concept is this, my friend: if you are stranded on an island, of course the only thing you would want is a bag of Le Chat Gourmet."

Mr. Green nodded approvingly.

Monsieur Bertrand's assistant placed me next to the bag of Le Chat Gourmet and then arranged the models around me. Perhaps it was time for a career change, I thought. This was definitely easier on the eyes than being a spy.

"He looks so handsome," Veronique gushed.

I did look rather dashing, if I do say so myself. Several of the models purred at me.

"Are you ready, Monsieur Stink?" the photographer asked me.

I flicked my tail, and Monsieur Bertrand began snapping away.

"Turn to the camera, love the camera," Monsieur Bertrand was saying. "The camera is a bowl of delicious cat food."

I turned this way and that, looking straight into the camera.

"He is a natural!" Veronique declared.

Anya murmured in my ear, "Don't you just hate these avant-garde photographers?"

What was she talking about? I found the whole experience rather enjoyable.

Monsieur Bertrand lifted his camera and shouted, "Start the waterfall!"

Waterfall?

Suddenly, a torrent of water rained down, slamming into us with all the force of a tsunami. When I opened my eyes, choking, Monsieur Bertrand was still snapping away.

"Look at the camera, Monsieur Stink!" he shouted. "Look at the camera!"

Perhaps I would stick to spying after all.

3

Murder on the Cat Express

AFTER THE photo shoot, a pair of assistants toweled me off and ran a hair dryer over my fur. Veronique crouched down and smiled at me.

"You did a wonderful job, Monsieur Stink," she said. "We are all so happy with your work. Soon you will be the most famous cat in all of France." She stood and turned to Mr. Green. "And now your vacation begins."

Veronique presented the family with a detailed itinerary and a thick packet of train tickets.

"I think you will enjoy this very much," she said. "Your first stop is Bois de Perrault, a village in the mountains of southwest France, where the Le Chat Gourmet factory is. After that, you will be going to

Carcassonne, where the first Le Chat Gourmet spokes-cat, Bernard, was born. And then you will be going to the port city of Marseilles, where the fish for Le Chat Gourmet is purchased. The next three stops—"

"What?" Aaron asked in dismay. "We're visiting historic sites of a cat food company? Oh, puhleese."

"What about EuroDisney?" Lily said to Mr. Green, her eyes accusing. "You promised!"

"Come on, gang, it'll be fun," Mr. Green said enthusiastically. "I've always wanted to see where Le Chat Gourmet is made."

"There'd better be a pool," Mrs. Green muttered.

Our train was an overnight express, leaving Paris that evening. But we barely made it to the station on time as Mr. Green insisted on stopping at a local pet supply store to check out the French merchandise. He was thrilled to find a new type of collar.

"Will you look at this?" Mr. Green said, climbing back into our cab. He lifted a plastic collar with an antenna and a series of blinking lights on it.

"Cool. What is it, Dad?" my boy asked.

"I've never seen anything like it in America, not even at the cat shows. It's called a Cat Tracker 9000X. It can send a signal to this receiver box from over ten kilometers away," he said, squinting at the

French instruction manual. "Is that more or less than ten miles?"

Please. I was not impressed. A seasoned spy could disable a bug in seconds.

"Fasten your seat belt, honey," Mrs. Green said to her husband.

After a breakneck ride to the station in a French taxicab, we ran to our train, bags in tow.

"The cat must stay in the cage at all times," the conductor said as we boarded the train. Aaron was holding me in his arms.

I meowed at him. Couldn't he tell I was a cat of breeding?

"But Mr. Stink's famous," Aaron said.

"This is a train, not a petting zoo," the conductor sniffed.

"No duh," Aaron muttered.

"Aaron, behave," Mrs. Green said, and Lily snickered.

"If you prefer, we can stow your animal in the back with the luggage," the conductor said in a cool voice.

With the luggage? I meowed in outrage. This was no way to treat a celebrity!

"I know, sorry, Mr. Stink," Aaron said as he put me back in the cage. "This whole trip is lame," he whispered to me, and for once, I had to agree.

The train was crowded, and so the family was forced to split up. Mr. and Mrs. Green and Lily took seats at the front of the car while Aaron and I had a seat to ourselves near the back.

"Remember, Aaron. Our stop is Bois de Perrault," Mr. Green said as we made our way down the aisle.

"Least we don't have to listen to Lily whine," Aaron said to me happily, maneuvering my carrier onto the seat next to him.

I meowed and scratched at the latch of the cage.

"Okay, Mr. Stink. I'll let you out. But don't let the conductor see you, and no running off, okay?" He opened the cage, and I hopped out.

The train began to move, and I looked out the window at the passing French countryside, feeling nostalgic. Our first stop was not far from Chatterie la Colline Marguerite, the cattery where I had been spent my kittenhood.

I had often wondered about my heritage. I had been discovered in the woods just outside the cattery, and the owners had taken me in. It was very unusual. One simply didn't find purebred Bengal kittens wandering the forest. Because of this, the other kittens had teased me horribly, saying I had no pedigree. I used to dream of having a brother to protect me from the other kittens when they were mean.

Still, it hadn't been an altogether bad experience. Dame Marguerite, an older cat, had taken me under her paw and raised me as one of her litter. She would amuse us kittens with stories of Catlandia, the mythical kingdom of legend. I loved the Catlandia tales of King Artfur and the Great Round Food Dish.

The rocking of the train combined with the excitement of the last few days was too much. I found myself drifting off, dreaming of my kittenhood days.

I awoke abruptly. It was just before dawn. A strange current in the air was making my whiskers quiver.

A staticky voice came over the loudspeaker, "*Mesdames et messieurs*. Next stop Bois de Perrault in one half hour."

A shadow fell across me and I leaped to the side, just in time to avoid a large suitcase slamming with a heavy thud onto the seat where I had been a moment ago. The luggage sprang open, and ladies underwear flew out in all directions.

"Wha—Mr. Stink, what's going on?" Aaron asked groggily.

I glanced up to the overhead luggage rack to see a black shape speeding toward the back of the train. A *cat-sized* black shape with a long, furry tail. I dashed after him.

"Where do you think you're going, Mr. Stink! Hey—stop!" Aaron cried.

But I couldn't stop to explain. I had an assassin to catch.

The next car back was a sleeper car. My assailant had vanished without a trace. *Clearly a trained professional,* I thought, which meant that someone had hired him to take me out. Had Macavity's minions followed me all the way to France?

I padded quietly along the narrow aisle against the windows, but there was no sign of him. On the right, thin doors led into private cabins where passengers could relax and sleep. Some of the doors were propped open. I peeked carefully inside the first one.

A family of Japanese tourists were sprawled out across the cabin, all sleeping quietly. No sign of any cats here.

The second cabin was full of young French schoolchildren wearing uniforms, apparently on a class outing.

"Regardez le p'tit miew-miew!" one of the girls squealed.

As a cat who had spent his kittenhood in France, I knew exactly what this little girl said, and it did not bode well:

Look at the little kitty!

Her friend tried to grab my tail. Soon all the children

were trying to catch me as I raced around the small cabin, leaping on and off luggage to avoid being captured by their grimy fingers. A large boy blocked the door with an evil grin, but I executed a skillful leap through his legs and scampered out the door. I raced down the hall, thankful that I had escaped intact. Truly, some of the evil villains I had locked paw with didn't hold a candle to schoolchildren!

Then I saw the shadow: something with four legs was moving around inside the next cabin.

I have you now! I thought.

I puffed my fur out and rushed in, hoping to surprise my foe. But I was in for surprise myself. On the other side of the door was not the black cat, but a large and irritable Doberman Pinscher.

The dog growled low in his throat the instant he saw me.

Sorry. My mistake, sir, I said, backing away and smoothing down my fur. *Wrong cabin.*

You haf zat right, cat! he snarled with a German accent and lunged for me.

Abruptly, the dog was yanked back on a leash.

"Brutus, sit!" his human barked in German.

I didn't wait around to see if Brutus had attended obedience school but beat a hasty exit. I was just catching my breath when I saw the conductor enter the rear of the car. I sincerely doubted the assassin had made it past his keen eyes.

There was a blur of movement at the other end of the car. The black cat met my gaze tauntingly, then turned tail and ran back the way we had just come. I dashed after him. Aaron was in the aisle, heading toward us.

"Mr. Stink, you can't run around in the train! The conductor will get you!" he said.

The black cat flashed me an evil grin and leaped onto one of the backs of the seats. I leaped right after him, and Aaron pursued both of us. I bounded from seat to seat, snagging more than one person's hat with my claws as I passed. Occupational hazard.

"Mr. Stink, stop horsing around!" he called.

The assassin jumped onto the luggage rack again, and I followed suit.

"Mr. Stink, what the—?"

The black cat disappeared through a vent in the roof of the car.

And I went after him.

On top of the train, the assassin was padding sure-footedly toward the rear.

I tried to follow him, but the wind was so strong that I thought I might blow off. I crouched low and inched onward slowly. I soon saw why the black cat was having less trouble than I. He was leaving sticky black pawprints behind him.

He must have crossed through a patch of tar on the roof that I hadn't seen. Had he planned his escape route all along?

By now, I had completely lost sight of him. I couldn't go back against the wind; I could only keep going. I flattened my ears and pressed on. I had to cross two cars before I found another open roof vent. I poked my head through and saw huge piles of luggage everywhere. I hopped down, using the luggage as steps.

The rear door was open, and a ticket collector stood at a rail smoking a cigarette. From his relaxed pose, I deduced he hadn't seen the assassin pass this way. But before I could turn around, a set of sharp claws stung me on the cheek. I whirled and fell back, tumbling into a stack of hatboxes, but I was on my feet in an instant. The black cat and I circled each other slowly.

"Who are you working for?" I demanded.

He smirked and licked my blood from his claws.

Without warning, he charged at me and bowled me over. The two of us rolled toward the back of the train.

"Mon Dieu!" shouted the ticket collector, finally noticing us.

He tried to dodge out of the way and accidentally stepped on the black cat's tail. Fortunately, that got the assassin off of me. Unfortunately, I rolled right off the back of the train and onto the tracks.

Even with four legs, it was a long walk to Bois de Perrault.

I reached our hotel in the late afternoon. It wasn't hard to locate; it was the only one in town. I was bruised and scratched from my tumble from the train, the pads of my feet were raw, and I had burs stuck to my fur. All in all, I didn't exactly look like Le Chat Gourmet. Not to mention I was exhausted and starving.

I found my boy staring worriedly out the window of his third-floor room. I meowed up at him loudly to get his attention.

"Shh!" he said, looking over his shoulder. "I'll be right down."

He ushered me inside and up to his room.

"Where have you been?" he demanded after he closed the door.

Walking across half of France, I wanted to say.

He pointed at the cage, where a towel had been carefully sculpted into a cat-shaped lump. "I had to cover for you. I thought you were gone forever!"

I'd never abandon my boy, I thought. Didn't he know that?

"Can you imagine how much trouble I would get into if I lost you? Especially with this whole Cat Gourmet thing going on? Dad would kill me, chop me up into little pieces, and feed me to the piranhas in the shop. Not to mention I'd be grounded for a million years!"

I hung my head contritely.

"Promise me you won't run away again," he said.

I meowed to assure him I would do no such thing, but he still didn't look happy. I rubbed up against him, purring.

"Humph," he said. "I should put you in your cage right now."

But I could sense him softening and rubbed my nose into his hand.

"All right, all right," he said, and scratched me behind the ears. "You're a mess." He started to pluck the burs out of my fur. "What did you get into, anyway?"

I sighed. I just hoped he had remembered to pack my brush.

4

The Castle of a Thousand Cats

WELL, THAT was certainly exciting," Mrs. Green said, not sounding the least bit excited. "Now where's the pool?"

We had just finished our tour of the Le Chat Gourmet factory. While my humans were not particularly impressed, I had enjoyed myself immensely. I had been given several tastings of the new flavors. I had no doubt that the new braised veal variety would be a hit on both sides of the Atlantic.

"Yeah, Dad, where's the pool?" Aaron piped up.

"Don't you want to see the castle that inspired the creation of Le Chat Gourmet?" Mr. Green asked.

"No!" Lily said. "I want to go to the pool."

"Castle?" Aaron asked, intrigued. "With real swords and everything?"

"Yep," Mr. Green said, consulting the itinerary. "It's an old one. From 1276."

"Cool," Aaron said. "Let's go see that."

"And then the pool," Mrs. Green said.

We piled back into the rental car and set off down a country lane. Aaron held me on his lap. Fearing that I would run away again, my boy had made me wear the extremely uncomfortable tracking collar. It had a little antenna sticking out from the top that kept banging into everything.

"Not far now," Mr. Green said. "There's the sign for Ferme-de-la-Vallée. That's where the castle is."

Ferme-de-la-Vallée? My heart leaped! The cattery where I had been adopted by Sir Archibald was just outside Ferme-de-la-Vallée!

Indeed, we drove right by the entrance for the cattery on our way down the lane. It looked the same as I remembered, with the large stone columns and a formal sign marking the entrance.

CHATTERIE LA COLLINE MARGUERITE

ÉLEVAGE DES CHATS EXCEPTIONNELS

The Daisy Hill Cat Farm, breeders of exceptional cats. *Perhaps I could sneak off and visit it tonight,* I thought. See if any of the old grandames were still around.

We reached the castle moments later. Or rather, what was left of it.

"I thought you said this was a castle," Aaron groused. "This is just a pile of rubble."

The ruins of what was once a great castle lay in heaps around us. There was a keep and a tower that looked as if it would fall over at any moment. But it was not these images that set my whiskers tingling. I sensed . . . cats. A *lot* of cats.

"Would you look at that," Mr. Green said, pointing.

Six cat tails disappeared into the rubble.

"There's some more over there," Aaron said.

Ten more cats scattered and vanished.

"It's a real cat castle," Mr. Green teased. "I could do some business in this place, huh, Mr. Stink?"

An elderly man, a caretaker, walked up to us then. *"Bonjour!"*

"Uh, *bonjour,*" Mr. Green said, horribly mangling the word. "You sure do have a lot of stray cats living here, huh?"

"Mais oui," the man said. "The story is told that the

baron who built this castle had a great fondness for cats, because they rescued his infant son from wolves. Now they guard his ruins. Also"—he winked—"I leave food out for them." He looked down at me, his eyes narrowing. "That is a fine cat you have. The Bengal is the most noble of cats."

Mr. Green brightened. "Mr. Stink here is the spokescat for Le Chat Gourmet!"

"My goodness! A celebrity!" the man said. "Pleased to meet you, Monsieur Stink."

"Is there anything cool to see around here?" Aaron interrupted.

The old man turned to my boy. "The museum in town has all manner of weapons that were discovered in these very ruins. Swords as big as you!"

"Swords?" Aaron's eyes bulged. "Can we go to the museum, huh, Dad?"

The sun was setting over the countryside.

"It's getting pretty late. Why don't we go there tomorrow?" Mr. Green suggested.

We were heading back to the parking lot when I felt my hackles rise.

Sitting on the hood of our car was the black cat!

He took off toward the ruins, leaping over a crumbling wall.

"Mr. Stink!" Aaron said sharply. "Where do you think you're going?"

I looked at him in astonishment. Wasn't it perfectly clear where I was going? A spy must be proactive about security.

"Don't you remember our conversation last night?" he asked me.

"You guys stayed up late talking?" Mrs. Green said with a smile. "Mr. Stink looks like a cat who has a few stories."

If she only knew.

"Come on, Mr. Stink," Aaron said, holding open the car door.

I sighed and hopped into the car.

I sat perched in the window of the hotel room, looking out at the night. Judging from the soft snores coming from the bed, my boy was fast asleep. With an assassin on the loose, I was not about to sleep. I could take catnaps when the humans were awake.

Bois de Perrault was a picturesque medieval village with narrow winding streets. It was a beautiful night, the smell of braised rabbits in red wine and mushroom sauce lingering in the air. All was quiet and still.

In the street below, a dark creature slithered out of the shadows. Who else? The assassin cat.

He looked up at my window and raised an eyebrow, taunting me. It was obviously a trap. But I preferred to deal with him now, on my own terms.

The window lock was laughably low-tech. I would have no trouble getting out.

I looked at Aaron. He was sleeping soundly. I didn't want to disobey him, but I would be back in no time. He would never even know I had been gone.

Carefully, I put my paw on the window latch and used my weight. The handle turned easily, and the window opened. I followed the roofline to an adjacent building that was lower, and then another one and another until I could jump to an awning and down to the street. The black cat was sitting across the street under a lamp, waiting for me. Rather sportsmanlike for an assassin.

I strolled right up to him. He nodded.

"Who are you working for?" I asked.

"Wouldn't you like to know," he said.

"Does he want a meeting, or do you have some ridiculous trap laid for me?" I drawled.

"Follow me and find out," the assassin taunted, and jumped into an open sewer.

I sighed. Just once it would be nice to chase down a criminal and not end up smelling like garbage. My name was bad enough. But what choice did I have?

I leaped after him into the darkness.

5

Bats in the Belfry

I **RACED AFTER** the sound of splashing pawsteps.

In short order, I found myself wading in mucky water up to my knees. I skidded to a stop at a fork in the tunnel and slipped. I came up sputtering to see a sewer rat watching in amusement.

"'E went zataway," the rat said, snickering.

Really, if this assassin was trying to torture me, he was doing a bang-up job.

Moments later, I was back on the streets. Rainwater dripped from the gutters overhead.

Rainwater?

I glanced up. The cat was on the rooftops, sewer water dripping from his fur.

Wooden scaffolding leaned against an old church that was being restored. I raced up a series of ramps and continued after him, following the wet pawprints up the roof to a small belfry where a number of copper bells hung.

A high-pitched squeal was my only warning. The fluttering of wings filled my ears, and something leathery brushed past me in the dark.

There were bats in the belfry!

"Abandon all hope, you who disturb our rest," a voice squeaked ominously.

I shook my head in disgust. Bats are ridiculous creatures. They like to think of themselves as some great terror that stalks the night, but in truth they're nothing more than clumsy rodents with wings. The Germans have it right: their word for "bat" is *Fledermaus*. "Flying mouse."

"Look at the size of that bug!" another voice chirped, pitched so high I could barely hear it.

Generally speaking, bats are nothing to fear, but this lot had wild, bloodshot eyes and were foaming at the mouth. Rabies. Now I had something to worry about.

"I'm not a bug," I said soothingly. "Why don't you all just go back to sleep?"

"A giant talking bug! Those are the best kind!" Sharp little teeth gleamed all about me in the darkness.

"Get him!"

All at once, they swarmed me, and I batted them away, no pun intended. I ducked my head low to keep the tips of my ears from being nipped off.

I ran through the belfry, dodging left and right, and onto the other side of the roof. Immediately, all four feet went out from under me as I slipped on a patch of moss. I slid down the roof, scrambling to gain purchase on the slate tiles, but it was useless. I tumbled over the edge and barely managed to get one claw on a gargoyle. I looked down.

Below me was an immense wagon of hay. I could see the black cat just jumping down from it.

I let go.

I dug myself out of the hay and looked around. I was in a deserted market square. There were closed-up stalls and piles of garbage. The aroma of day-old fish wafted through the air.

The black cat could be hiding anywhere.

A clattering sound to my left gave him away, and I darted around a crate of rotting tomatoes. Suddenly, three strange-looking creatures appeared out of nowhere and surrounded me.

The black-spotted animals had long, catlike tails,

muscular bodies, and slender triangular heads with short whiskers. If anything, they looked like a missing link between a rat and a Bengal cat. But they were not cats—they were called genets. And judging from the numerous notches in their ears, they were not from the Bois de Perrault tourist board.

I looked past them to see the assassin standing there. He flashed me a grin. A trap.

"You got away from us last time, but you're on your last life, Furrdinand," one of the genets snarled.

Furrdinand?

Another one screeched with laughter. "We are really going to enjoy sinking our claws into you."

Now, genets are quite small compared to a full-grown Bengal, but they can be vicious and extremely fast. I had tangled with their kind years ago. Three of them at once would be too much for an ordinary cat, but I was an expert in paw-to-paw combat.

In a flash, they bared their teeth and rushed at me. I rolled onto my back and flipped the first one toward a vegetable stand. He crashed through a crate of moldy carrot ends.

The second one leaped at me. It was a clumsy attack, and I dispatched him with a swift kick. He went tumbling into a pile of rancid fish heads.

"Choke on those bones," I said. I turned to the remaining genet.

He looked left and right at his groaning associates. "I think I need back-up," he said. He made a break for it.

"Not so fast," I countered. "You and I have unfinished business." I knocked over the wooden post that was holding up an awning above us. Thick canvas came crashing down, and I rolled to safety.

The genet yowled and struggled but only succeeded in tangling himself more.

"Ta-ta," I said. "I'd stay for tea, but I have a prior engagement." I turned to look at the assassin.

His face fell. He turned tail and ran.

I trailed the assassin out of town and into a thick forest. My new radio collar quickly became a problem. The hard plastic bounced painfully against my neck as I raced over the rough terrain. And I nearly strangled myself several times when the antenna snagged on brambles and low branches.

I started to fall behind. But my mark was leaving a trail of broken twigs and crushed leaves that was kitten's play to follow, even in the dark. He was no match for my expert tracking skills.

At long last, I broke through into a clearing. The

black cat was on the other side, his head down, panting.

"All right," he said. "I give up. You're too fast for me."

I chuckled. "Who sent you?" I asked, advancing on him.

Suddenly, the ground went out from under me, and I felt myself falling. Contrary to popular belief, cats do not always land on their feet. I sprawled on my rear with a thump and felt a crunch. The plastic cat collar had snapped. I easily pawed it off my neck.

So much for that annoyance.

I looked up. I was at the bottom of a deep pit. This, then, was the real trap.

"Seems I have the last laugh," the assassin gloated, smirking down at me from the edge. "I wonder how long it would take you to starve to death down there," he mused.

"Long enough to break out of here and wring your scrawny neck," I growled, taking a step forward. I winced at the sudden pain in my back foot. I must have injured it in the fall.

The black cat pressed his lips together. "Hmm. Precisely." He stepped back from the rim of the pit, disappearing from view. A shower of twigs and dirt rained down on me. "Which is why," he called down, "I plan to fill in the pit right now." Another shower of dirt rained down, and I spat.

"Dog. Who are you working for?" I demanded. "You might as well tell me if I'm going to be buried alive."

The cat's head reappeared over the edge. "Oh, I suppose you're right. In fact, I'm sure he'd want you to know his name is—*urk.*"

There was a thud. Another cat's head appeared over the rim. A Bengal!

"Your Highness!" the cat cried.

6

My Old Friend Porthos

THE BENGAL kicked some long leafy branches down into the pit and helped me scrabble my way up. The black cat lay on his side near the edge, unconscious. My rescuer had knocked him out, it seemed.

"Thanks," I panted.

The other cat laughed heartily. "Typical. Rescued yet again by your old friend Porthos. Ah, Your Highness, you never change, do you?" He laughed again and swatted me on the shoulder.

Why was everyone calling me Your Highness lately? I was starting to get a feeling that this had nothing to do with being Le Chat Gourmet.

"Well," I said, trying to fill the uncomfortable silence. "I really ought to be getting back."

"It's about time," the other cat said. "Your little adventures are all very well and good, but you're starting to neglect your duties at court."

"Court?"

Porthos seemed puzzled. "Did you by any chance strike your head when you fell?"

"Uh, no," I said. "Just my back foot."

"Who was the cat who attacked you?" he asked.

"I haven't the faintest idea. I haven't had time to interrogate him."

In the same instant, we both looked over to where the black cat lay.

He was gone!

I took a step forward and yowled in pain.

Porthos was at my side in an instant. "Let's attend to your wound. I'll send the Royal Guards after him, although I have little hope they will catch him."

As we walked along—well, limped in my case— Porthos asked, "Did none of my messengers reach you, Your Highness?"

"Uh, no," I said, deciding to play along with it. "We must have missed each other. Paris is a big city."

"No matter, you've returned just in time." He

hesitated. "Your mother, Queen Furrypaws, is quite ill."

"Ill?"

He nodded gravely. "Lord Ratsputin has been caring for her. Your father's death still lies heavily upon her, and Lord Ratsputin has been helping her try to make contact with his spirit."

"Has he?" I said.

I had run into several cats with supposed mystical powers during my time with Sir Archibald. Every single one of them had turned out to be a fake. Still, I could understand *wanting* to believe. What I wouldn't give to be able to talk to Sir Archibald again!

"She will be very happy to see you," he said.

"Where exactly are we going?" I asked.

"To Catlandia, of course," Porthos said, giving me a strange look.

"I'm sorry. Did you say *Catlandia*?" I asked.

"Are you certain you didn't strike your head when you fell, Your Highness?"

Maybe I *had* struck my head, and this was all a dream.

Dawn was breaking, and light filtered through the thick trees. We reached a ridge, and Porthos stopped. I looked down. We were at the ruined castle on the hill that I had visited with the Greens.

Porthos gave a great yowl, calling, "Felines of Catlandia, your Crown Prince has returned! All hail His Royal Highness, Prince Furrdinand!"

I couldn't believe it.

Catlandia was a dump.

Hundreds of scrawny stray cats appeared from nowhere. They sat along the tumbledown walls, bowing their heads respectfully as we passed.

"The Prince has returned!" they meowed.

One cat, a lovely female domestic shorthair, burst from the crowd and laid a dead bird at my feet. "Your Highness! We are so happy you're back!"

All these cats thought I was this Prince Furrdinand character. *He must be a handsome fellow,* I thought.

I followed Porthos into the tower and up a crumbling flight of stairs to what had once been the tower room. At the far end, an elderly female Bengal sat curled on a pile of old, moth-eaten blankets, surrounded by attendants. Queen Furrypaws, I assumed. A cat with silvery blue fur, a Russian Blue, sat close to the Queen's ear, whispering to her. Was this Ratsputin?

A great hush fell over the room when I entered.

The jig is up, I thought. *Surely the Queen will recognize her own offspring.*

"My son!" she meowed weakly.

Apparently not.

I walked toward her slowly, my head bowed in respect. I stopped a courteous distance from her throne of blankets, but she leaned toward me and touched her nose to mine affectionately.

"Oh, you are home," she said in a misty voice. "Never stay away for so long again. We feared we had lost you as we lost your father."

Stunned at this warm welcome, I glanced past her at the Russian Blue. The cat stared at me, pale.

He looked as if he'd seen a ghost.

7

It's Good to Be the Prince

IT **WAS** clear that everyone, including the Queen,
thought I was Crown Prince Furrdinand.

The question was: how long did I have before the
real Prince came back and had me skinned alive for
impersonating him? And, of course, there was the
little question of who the black cat assassin was
working for and why he was after me. Until I could
answer the second question, I decided I could risk
ignoring the first. After all, it's handy to have a
palace full of bodyguards when an assassin is out to
get you.

After my meeting with the Queen, Porthos ushered
me down a crumbling set of stairs.

"Where are we going?" I asked as casually as I could. He gave me an odd look. "To your chambers, Your Highness, where your grooms can attend to your injury. Why, did you have somewhere else in mind?"

"No, no," I said quickly. "That will be fine."

We rounded a corner, and a cute young cat with thick, woolly fur flung herself at me.

"Furrdinand!" she cried. "Welcome home!"

She was a Chartreux, if I was not mistaken, with a sturdy body and short legs. In fact, she looked rather like a potato propped up on four toothpicks. Not my type, really, although one had to admit she had a wholesome glow, lovely eyes, and an adorable face.

"Camille," Porthos said coolly.

"Captain Porthos," she replied, equally cool. She turned to me. "You had me worried sick. Why did you disappear for so long this time?"

"Well, I, er . . . needed a break."

She rolled her eyes. "You always say that."

"Do I?" I asked.

"This is no time for jokes, Furrdinand," she said, sounding cross. She looked around furtively and then lowered her voice. "Lord Ratsputin has made himself indispensable to the Queen. No one may speak to her without going through him, not even me, and I am her cat-in-waiting. And now Papa has gone missing."

"Missing?"

"Yes," she said. "Lord Ratsputin says he sent him off on an errand of great importance, but Papa would never leave without telling me. Have you seen him?"

I hesitated. "I'm not sure."

"Not sure?" Her eyes grew wide. "Did you see him or didn't you?"

"I can't recall," I said. "I'm not exactly myself at the moment."

"Oh, Furrdinand, you're impossible!" she cried, and ran off.

Porthos chuckled. "Still have a way with the ladies, I see."

He led me to a small room that had been formed by falling walls. There a bevy of lovely female cats awaited me.

"Your Highness," they cooed, bowing their heads.

"What is this?" I whispered to Porthos.

"Your grooms, of course, sir."

"Riiiight," I said. "Nice to see you all again."

"Now just relax, Your Highness, and we shall take care of everything," one of the lady cats murmured. She was a lovely Balinese.

What followed was more delightful than a bowl of fresh cream. The Balinese skillfully kneaded my sore leg with her paws while another of the lady cats chewed the burs and brambles out of my fur. A third gave me a pawdicure: she carefully cleaned my paws, nibbling away any flakes that had split from my claws.

I purred in delight.

Even the most hard-bitten counterspy enjoys a bit of rest and relaxation on occasion, and heaven knew this "holiday" had been anything but relaxing so far. I closed my eyes and let my troubles melt away. It was almost as nice as getting a good brushing from Aaron.

I felt a pang of guilt. No doubt my boy had discovered I was missing by now. Still, I reasoned, I would not remain here long. I simply needed to track down the assassin.

"Caviar, Your Highness?" one of the ladies asked.

I could get used to this.

After a well-deserved catnap, I felt like my normal dashing self. I followed Porthos up the winding tower stairs to a hall where supper was already in progress. He stopped me outside the room.

"Be careful what you eat and drink, Furrdinand," he

cautioned in low tones. I thought I could hear the faint squeaking of rats in the distance.

"What do you mean?"

"I've been quietly investigating your father's death on my own time," he said. "Lord Ratsputin has forbidden any inquiries into the subject. He says your father's spirit does not wish the crime to be investigated. Still, I cannot help but suspect he had something to do with the King's untimely demise."

"And why is that?"

"A Bengal cat in the prime of his life does not simply drop dead after eating a sardine."

"You suspect he was poisoned?" I asked. I knew of another cat who had made my life a nightmare through the use of poison. *Could Ratsputin have some connection to Macavity?* I wondered.

"We'll talk of this later. We must be careful." He nodded and whispered, "The walls have ears."

Something smelled rotten in the kingdom of Catlandia.

We arrived at a large hall whose ceiling had collapsed a long time ago. Soft green grass covered the space between the walls. Cats lounged about, feasting on bowls of food left out by the groundskeeper. In addition, it seemed that the tourists and local towns-people followed a custom of leaving bits of food.

"My son," Queen Furrypaws meowed. "Come, sit by me."

For this evening's menu, the palace chef had scavenged some fried fish sticks, part of a hamburger, and a ham and cheese sandwich. My patrons at Le Chat Gourmet would not have approved.

All during supper, Ratsputin hovered on the other side of the Queen, swaying his cobralike head from side to side and leaning forward to point out the choicest bits of food for her.

The Russian Blue is an unusual breed. Rumored to be the descendants of the royal cat of the Russian czars, they possess a distinct silvery blue coat, green eyes, and one other unique trait—they look as if they are smiling all the time. In the case of Ratsputin, I felt certain that the ever-present smile hid something sinister.

"The Queen and I have been so worried about you, Your Highness," he said in a solicitous voice. His fur shimmered in the dim light, shifting from gray to silver to blue. I could see why some might think that he would have magical powers. "Where have you been all this time?"

I decided I might as well stick with the story I already had. "Paris."

His green eyes glittered strangely and . . . did his smile slip for a moment? There was more to this cat than met the eye. "Did you see any *krisi?*"

I blinked. *Krisi?*

Krisi was Russian for "rats." Languages are a spy's business, and I speak Russian just as fluently as English and French, having catnapped many times in the language classrooms at MI9. Even so, Russian was not a common language among French cats, and the way he had said it, with a strange emphasis, also puzzled me.

"One or two," I said cautiously. "Why do you ask?"

"I am merely concerned for His Highness's safety," he said, looking annoyed.

"So the infallible Ratsputin is not always right, after all," the Queen said, laughing lightly. Her laugh turned to a cough, and Ratsputin hurried to her side. "Ratsputin had a vision."

"Your Highness," the Russian Blue demurred, "my visions are but whispers of the future."

"He said you drowned!" She dissolved into another fit of coughing.

"Must have been another prince," I said dryly.

"Perhaps it is a future yet to come," Ratsputin intoned ominously. "I would advise you to avoid water."

I sniffed at my water dish and remembered Porthos's warning about poison.

"After all," Ratsputin murmured in a voice that only I could hear, "my visions have a way of coming true when you least expect it."

8

The Cream Thickens

THE NEXT morning, Porthos brought me to the throne room.

In the hallway outside, cats were lined up waiting to get in to see the Queen. A pair of Bengals—Royal Guards—lounged scowling on either side of the entrance.

"On your feet!" Porthos hissed at them. "Stand at attention for your Prince!"

The cats complied slowly, as if dazed or drunk.

"What's wrong with them?" I whispered out of the side of my mouth.

"All my Guardscats are like this lately." His whiskers twitched in frustration. "It's as if they are under a spell.

They are now loyal only to Ratsputin."

Interesting. I recalled supper the night before, how Ratsputin had stared at me, almost as if he were trying to hypnotize me. Perhaps that was the secret to Ratsputin's so-called sorcery. Fortunately, I was immune to hypnosis: it was one of the many interrogation techniques I had learned how to resist at MI9.

Inside the hall, Queen Furrypaws was sitting on her cat bed acting as judge in various disputes. Ratsputin was at her side. A number of kittens-in-waiting also attended her, and Camille was among them as a chaperone. I nodded to her, but she wouldn't meet my eyes. Apparently, she was still annoyed with me.

It soon became clear that Ratsputin was doing all the judging. The Queen was not making any decisions and appeared to be ill, or napping, or both.

"Two fish heads," Ratsputin was saying.

"But I already paid my taxes," a small, scruffy-looking cat said.

"Are you questioning the authority of the Queen?" Ratsputin demanded in a low growl. The Queen appeared to stir, and one eyelid flickered.

"Of course not, yer lordship," the cat replied, cowering.

I turned to Porthos. "How long has this been going on?"

"There have been many changes while you were away, sir."

"I can see that. Good thing I'm back," I said, and I sauntered up to the throne. Ratsputin seemed surprised to see me.

"Your Highness," he said. "What are you doing here?"

"I thought I'd give Mother a paw with some of these cases," I said.

"You need not concern yourself," he said, staring at me intently. "I can take care of everything. *Yesss. I can take care of everything.*"

His voice was low and soothing, humming in my ears. His eyes seemed to grow bigger and bigger. I felt certain I could hear the faint squeaking of rats in the distance. . . .

"Listen to *krisi*," he whispered.

That word again! He *was* trying to hypnotize me.

Sometimes hypnotists will use a form of mind control called a posthypnotic suggestion. They will use a special trigger word—a word not likely to be used in everyday life—that will instantly put the subject into a suggestible state. *Krisi* certainly qualified as a word no cat of Catlandia would use in ordinary conversation.

In short, Ratsputin really *had* cast a spell over the Queen, the Royal Guards, and who knew how many other cats of Catlandia! Now he was trying to control me. Except he didn't know whom he was dealing with here.

"Actually," I said cheerfully, "I find these cases very interesting."

Ratsputin gave me an astonished look, and I blinked back innocently.

"You do?" Queen Furrypaws said, her eyes snapping open. "Oh, that's wonderful, son! You always hated sitting in judgment."

"Well, something about it interests me today."

The Queen struggled to stand. "In that case, I think I shall go take a nap. I am so very tired lately. Ratsputin?"

Ratsputin hesitated, looking at me, and then scurried to her side. As the two of them left, I heard it again: the distinct but very faint squeaking of rats. I shook my head. No one else seemed to hear anything.

I got down to business. I heard cases involving stolen food, kittens fighting with littermates, and one rather strange dispute involving a field mouse who was accusing a cat of eating all the berries in his winter stores. Finally, I found myself presiding over a case brought by two old mangy-looking cats. One of the cats claimed that the other cat had given him a case of fleas. The other cat insisted it was the other way around.

"So you see, Yer Majesty," the toothless old cat was saying. "I wouldn't have these here fleas if he hadn't slept in my bed."

"It's *my* bed, and I didn't give you no fleas! You gave 'em to me!" the other cat hissed. He was missing one eye.

"You flea-bitten old tom!" the old cat yowled.

"*You're* the flea-bitten old tom!" the other one hissed.

"Enough!" I shouted them down.

"The Queen usually tells them to come back when they have a real dispute," Porthos whispered to me, but I motioned him to be silent.

I glanced down the hill to a stream that divided in two, flowed on either side of the ruin as a natural moat, and joined together again on the downstream side.

"As it is unclear who gave the fleas to whom," I said, "we shall resolve this case in the following manner. See the moat down below?"

The old cats nodded warily.

"The two of you are to swim across the moat. Whoever reaches the other side first shall be declared the winner in this case," I announced.

The two old cats looked at each other and then ran off as fast as their old legs could toward the stream.

"Why are you having them swim across the moat, Your Majesty?" Porthos asked.

"Simple. To get rid of their fleas." I winked.

Porthos laughed and shook his head. I grinned back and looked over at Camille.

She was staring at me with an odd expression on her face.

I headed out to the castle grounds for a bit of fresh air, my duties as judge finished for the day. Some tourists were being led around by the elderly groundskeeper. I heard a young boy's voice, and I bounded onto a pile of rubble to get a better look. Aaron?

But no, it was only a young French boy in a school uniform. He was chasing after one of the cats I had sent to swim the moat. No wonder the subjects of Catlandia had run to hide when the Greens and I had visited.

"Your Highness," a voice purred next to me. "That was very well done."

It was Camille. The sun was setting, and she looked adorable in the golden light.

"No rest for a prince," I said lightly. In truth, being Furrdinand was beginning to wear on me. Like Sir Archibald always said, it was hard staying in deep cover.

"Then I'd say it's about time we had some fun," Camille replied saucily. "Care to go catch some rats with me?"

Now, I am not ordinarily a fan of rodent hunting. But I recalled that Chartreux are known to be excellent mousers, and perhaps this was something Camille and Furrdinand did often. "Why not?" I said with a shrug.

The moment the words left my mouth, I knew I had made a mistake.

Camille's expression darkened. "Funny, because the real Furrdinand doesn't like chasing rats. In fact, he's terrified of them." She narrowed her eyes. "Who are you?"

It seemed I was not the only one who smelled something rotten in the kingdom of Catlandia.

9

The Promise

BEFORE I could answer, she had me pressed up against a wall, unsheathed claws at my throat.

"What have you and your rat master done with my Furrdinand?" she growled.

My, what a feisty girl! I was beginning to like her more and more.

"If you're referring to Ratsputin," I said calmly, "I can assure you I'm not working for him."

She lowered her claws reluctantly. "Then who are you?"

"The name is Bristlefur. James Edward Bristlefur. Call me James," I said with a bow. "What gave me away?"

"Furrdinand hates court life. You seemed to enjoy it. Not to mention, you were, well, good."

"Really?" I asked, pleased.

"It is a remarkable resemblance," she said.

"I'm surprised Porthos hasn't caught on," I said.

"Porthos? Please," she sniffed. "That cat's all muscles and no brains."

"What do you have against Porthos?"

"He doesn't think I'm good enough for Furrdinand. Tradition dictates that Furrdinand marry a Bengal to keep the bloodline pure. Ooh, it's so infuriating." She stamped a paw. "Enough about Porthos. Where is Furrdinand?"

"I suspect he may be in some danger," I said, and explained to her about the assassin and the genets. "Tell me more about this Ratsputin character."

"No one really knows where he came from. My father was looking into his background when he disappeared."

There was a meow from above. We looked up to see Porthos on the crumbling battlements.

"Your Highness!" he called down. "You must come quickly!"

"What is it?" I asked.

"Your mother is dying!"

★ ★ ★

We followed Porthos up the steps of the crumbling tower to the Queen's chamber, passing through a phalanx of Royal Guards standing at attention. A rather fat Guardscat stood in the doorway, blocking our way.

"Stand aside, Athos," Porthos ordered.

The other cat didn't budge. "Strict orders from Lord Ratsputin. Let no one in," he intoned.

I leaned over to Athos and whispered in his ear. "The *krisi* say, 'Let them through.'"

He blinked and said, "Let them through."

It worked! I thought of something else.

"You won't tell Ratsputin we were here," I whispered in the cat's ear.

"I won't tell Ratsputin you were here," he repeated.

"Move along."

Athos waved a paw at us. "Move along."

As we entered the chamber, Porthos stared at me in wonder. "How did you do that?"

"Force is not always necessary," I said mysteriously.

Inside the chamber, the old Queen lay curled up in a ball on a pile of ratty-looking blankets. Her fur was matted and her breathing shallow. Ratsputin was nowhere in sight. We crept to her side and she opened her eyes.

"Furrdinand?" she rasped, her voice weak.

"I'm here," I said, moving closer.

"My son, you must do something for me," she said, trying to lift her head.

"Lie still," I urged her.

"Listen to me. You must go down to Ferme-de-la-Vallée and find Chatterie la Colline Marguerite," she said. "Tell Dame Marguerite that the hidden claw must be revealed."

The Daisy Hill Cat Farm? But that's where I grew up! And I knew Dame Marguerite very well. What was this all about?

"Promise me you'll do this," she whispered.

I looked into her cloudy eyes. They were kind, and I knew that Furrdinand, whoever he was, was lucky to have such a mother.

"I promise," I said.

Then the Queen closed her eyes and took a long, shuddering breath.

"The Queen is dead! Long live the King!" Porthos shouted.

We turned to see that a crowd had gathered in the archway to the chamber. The other cats took up the cry, "The Queen is dead! Long live the King!"

Holy cat litter—I was the King!

10

The Hidden Claw

KING OR not, I had a promise to keep. And a riddle to solve.

I got up early the next morning to avoid being seen. I was halfway across the bridge over the moat when I heard a feminine voice call out, "Where exactly do you think you're going . . . *James*?"

I gritted my teeth. "Go home, Camille. I work alone."

"You can't order me about. After all, you're not really the King." She grinned at me. "Besides, you're going to need my help. I know the area."

She had a point. "Very well," I conceded.

"This way is easier," she said, and I followed her down the mountain slope and into the thick forest.

"Where are you from?" she asked curiously.

"London," I replied. "Or I suppose I should say America now."

"What are you doing in France?"

"I am the new spokescat for Le Chat Gourmet," I said dryly.

"I love Le Chat Gourmet!" she gushed. "Sometimes the groundskeeper leaves it out for us."

It was my turn to ask a few questions. "Tell me about Furrdinand."

She pursed her lips. "You have to understand, his father, King Leopaw the Fifth, was very famous and much admired. He was the first cat since King Artfur to drive all the rats out of Catlandia."

"Impressive," I said. Inwardly, I thrilled to realize that the legends of Catlandia I had heard as a kitten were true.

"Very. Not to mention hard to live up to. Furrdinand doesn't think he could ever be as good a king as his father."

We had reached the edge of the forest. In the distance, across a field of daisies, I could see the familiar gates to Chatterie la Colline Marguerite. A wave of nostalgia washed over me as I saw the stone pillar with the leaping cat I remembered so clearly.

I started forward, but Camille hesitated. "What is it?" I asked.

"It's just that I've never been out of Catlandia. It's forbidden, you see," she said. "It's the only way to keep the secret safe."

"So stay here," I said, and plunged onward across the field of daisies.

"Wait!" Camille said, chasing after me.

We went around back to where the cats were kept. I had barely taken a step into the yard when I heard my name being called.

"James Edward Bristlefur, you scoundrel!"

Dame Marguerite was holding court with a group of kittens. No doubt teaching them the finer points of keeping one's claws in trim.

"Dame Marguerite!" I smiled. "You don't look a day over ten!"

Cat years, as you may know, are counted differently than human ones. Ten was quite a respectable middle age, although Dame Marguerite had been "ten" for many years.

"James!" she purred. "You look simply dashing, dear boy."

"How have you been, Dame Marguerite?"

Two kittens started hissing at each other. Without

warning, one struck out at the other with a paw. The other kitten retaliated with a smack, and soon they were rolling around in the dirt, yowling away.

She rolled her eyes. "This generation. They don't appreciate the finer points of education. You were always my best pupil. I knew you were destined for great things, James. Even as a kitten, you kept your tail up."

I smiled. Camille cleared her throat loudly.

"Who is your friend?" the Dame asked, raising a whisker.

"This is Camille," I said. "An, ahem, an associate of mine."

"A pleasure to meet you, Madame," Camille said with a bow.

"How charming," Dame Marguerite said, and turned to me. "Now tell me, James, why are you here? And before you say it's to visit me, remember that I could always tell when you were lying."

"To visit you, of course," I began. Dame Marguerite snorted, and I grinned devilishly. "I bring you a message from Catlandia."

"Catlandia?" She gave an uneasy laugh. "But everyone knows that's just a fairy tale."

"How curious," I said. "Since I've been there."

The expression on her face didn't change except for the telltale twitch of a whisker. She knew something.

"Queen Furrypaws is dead," I said.

"Dead?" she hissed with an indrawn breath.

I nodded. "And she told me to tell you that the hidden claw must be revealed."

She looked away, flicking her tail anxiously. "I never thought this day would come."

"What is this riddle?" I asked.

"There's no easy way to say this," she said with a sigh. "Queen Furrypaws was your mother."

Camille gasped.

Now, there are few things that can rattle an experienced international cat of mystery like myself, but this was one of them.

"What?" I finally stammered.

"There's one other thing," the Dame said. "You have an identical twin brother."

I stared at her, openmouthed. Not even when I faced Macavity had I been more at a loss for words.

"It's Furrdinand," she said.

"You always told me I was found in the forest, a lost orphan!"

"Well, technically, you *were* lost," the Dame said. "Let me explain. I snuck through that hole in the fence, you know the one—"

My jaw dropped in outrage. "But you always told us never—"

"Quiet," she said in a tone of voice that made me feel like a kitten again. "I was hunting in the forest, to keep my skills sharp, you know, dear, when all of a sudden I ran into a Bengal claiming to be the young Queen of Catlandia. How absurd! I thought she was mad, or worse. She was carrying a tiny blind kitten in her mouth by the scruff of its neck. She dropped it— *you*—at my feet and ran off, saying she would be back if the hidden claw should need to be revealed. What else was I to do? Of course I took you in. I've always thought of you as one of my own."

"But why? Why did she give me away?"

She looked down. "I don't know."

"I do," Camille said. "Soon after Queen Furrypaws gave birth to her litter, the kittens began dying. Some said they were poisoned. The Queen told everyone the only surviving male heir was Furrdinand."

"She hid me away to protect me," I finished. "But who was responsible?"

Camille shrugged. "The court of Catlandia has always been a litter box of intrigue. So many cats vying for the power of the cat bed."

"All these years," I said. "But for fate."

"Yes, but now you know the truth," Dame Marguerite said. "Cheer up. You have a brother. It's what you always wanted."

But I felt only a deep aching loneliness. For I had found my mother and lost her in the same day.

Back in Catlandia, Camille and I perched on a ruined wall as I wrestled with what to do. Did Macavity know that I was the hidden claw? Was he behind my brother's disappearance? And what about Ratsputin? Where did he fit in all this? Was he one of Macavity's operatives, or did he want the throne?

"Well, that explains why you look so much like Furrdinand. You really are the King then," Camille said glumly.

"Only if Furrdinand is dead."

Her whiskers quivered.

"I think for both our sakes we should assume that he's alive. We just have to find him," I said.

"Don't forget about my father. There has to be a connection."

"It does seem unlikely that both cats would go missing at the same time."

"By our custom, the coronation date is two days

from now," she said. "We need to find Furrdinand before then."

"Why the rush?"

"If you are actually crowned King, by our custom, it won't matter if we find him," she explained. "It could mean civil war!"

Two days. That wasn't much time.

A warning meow echoed through the air. "Humans! Humans!"

All around us, cats were dodging into hiding places in the ruins. Camille nudged me behind a rock, and we watched as a car pulled up.

"Tourists," Camille whispered. "The children are awful."

We crouched down low, listening as the voices wafted through the air. Mostly American by the sound of them. Then I heard a voice. A voice I knew well.

"Mr. Stink!" Aaron called. "Mr. Stink!"

I had to stop myself from running out into the open.

"Where are you, Mr. Stink?" my boy called. How I missed him!

"Mr. Stink, are you here?" Mr. Green called.

I risked a peek. He was looking haggard, and Aaron wasn't looking too well either. In fact, he looked positively grim.

"Come out, you no-good cat," Mrs. Green called.

"Hey, Mr. Stink!" Lily shouted.

Aaron was fiddling with his Cat Tracker. "I'm not getting a beep." He shook it in frustration. "Does this thing even work?"

"Mr. Stink can't have gone far," Mr. Green was saying to his son. "We'll just have to cancel the next part of the trip and keep looking."

"He's not here," Aaron said dismally. "He would have come when I called. I know he would have."

"We'll find him," Mr. Green promised, but he didn't sound very convincing. "Maybe they know something at the cat farm down the road."

I was torn. I wanted to run out and let Aaron know I was all right, but I had a duty to these cats to find Furrdinand. The Feline Code of Honor was something I lived by. After all, a cat without honor is no cat at all.

I had no choice. I had to continue the charade, no matter what the consequences.

"Mr. Stink!" Lily called one last time.

"Forget it," Aaron said.

As the Greens piled into the car, Camille turned to me. "Do you know who this Mr. Stink cat is?"

"Never heard of him," I said, and watched as the tiny car vanished into the distance.

11

The Cat in the Iron Collar

SOMETIME AFTER midnight, I awoke in Furr-dinand's chambers to the sound of rats squeaking.

Across the room, Porthos stood at attention in the doorway, but as I drew nearer, I could hear him snoring lightly. I took a breath and walked in front of him in perfect silence, but immediately, his breathing changed. Now here was a born Guardscat!

"Carry on, Porthos," I muttered soothingly.

"Mm, yes sir," he said, and began snoring again.

I peered out the doorway and saw the tail of a Blue Russian disappearing around a corner. It was Ratsputin, and he was up to something.

Hugging the shadows at the base of the walls, I followed him, careful to keep a respectable distance. At last, I felt in my element again: one of the first lessons taught to humans at MI9 is surveillance.

At a four-way junction, he looked around furtively and then scampered down a staircase. His ungroomed claws clicked on the stone floor. He slunk around a corner, but when I made the turn, he wasn't there. It was a dead end.

Was there something to the story of him being a sorcerer after all?

I examined the wall in front of me. There was a thirteenth-century fresco painted on it, a scene depicting the old baron in robes going on a pilgrimage accompanied by a brace of faithful cats looking ahead piously. But in the foreground, one of the cats stared straight out of the painting, one paw resting atop a very frightened-looking mouse.

Hmm.

I touched my paw to the mouse, and a section of the wall slid down, revealing a cat-sized secret passage! The old Baron must have installed this to allow his cats outside at night without him having to lower the drawbridge.

Genius.

I looked around to make certain I was not being followed and then plunged into darkness after Ratsputin.

I padded quietly down a curving set of stairs. The air grew dank, and I could hear the sound of dripping water. Still, the stairs descended. Finally, I heard the echoing sound of two voices not far below. I hesitated on a step, ears straining.

"Where's my prisoner? I don't care about this old tom. I want Furrdinand!" a voice said in low, ominous tones. Vaguely familiar ominous tones.

"He escaped," Ratsputin whined, his voice quivering. "I sent my best assassin after him and—"

"Escaped?" the other cat interrupted him.

"But he's come back. I will take care of it personally this time," Ratsputin said.

"Don't fail me again. You wouldn't want to find yourself missing an ear, would you? I have a tight schedule to keep," the other cat threatened. "Does Furrdinand suspect you?"

"No. I used the genets. But he's suspicious. If he discovers I was behind it, all our plans will be ruined."

I heard the sound of a smack and Ratsputin whimpering.

"Our plans? *My! My* plans!" the other cat said.

I leaned around the corner and looked below. Dim light from a grate above filtered down. I could just make out the form of Ratsputin cowering before a cat in the shadows, The cat's fluffy white paw was raised as if for another blow. And then I saw it.

He had six toes! I knew of only one polydactyl— that is, six-toed—cat with fluffy white fur.

Macavity.

I took a step toward them and my paw landed in a puddle.

Splash!

"You fool! You were followed!" Macavity hissed. He melted into the shadows.

"Sir?" Ratsputin whispered desperately in the darkness, whirling about.

But Macavity had vanished without a trace.

I leaped down the last few steps and faced the Blue Russian.

"I . . . Your Majesty," Ratsputin stammered. "I thought I heard meowing, so I came—"

"I heard everything, Ratboy. You might as well give yourself up."

A wild and angry gleam entered Ratsputin's eyes. He gave a high-pitched yowl. "*Krisi!* To me, to me!"

I was about to laugh and say *You have no power over me* when suddenly the damp air was filled with the sound of squeaking. Only this time, it grew louder and louder and *louder.*

Out of nowhere, dozens of rats appeared, forming a wall between the Blue Russian cat and me. He looked back at me, and his ever-present smile widened.

"Well, now that the cat is out of the bag, I am afraid I cannot let you live. Good-bye, Your Majesty." He turned and stalked off.

As one, the wall of rats surged toward me like a wave. With mighty sweeps of my paws, I tossed them aside, knocking them into channels of water that ran along each side of the vaulted chamber. They swam to safety, but more rats kept appearing, coming to take their place. Try as I might, I couldn't get through them or go after Ratsputin. He was gone. The rats were beginning to overwhelm me.

At that moment, a series of echoing meows came from the staircase. The rats turned in unison. Judging from the huge shadows thrown against the wall, it looked as if an entire cat army was descending the stairs!

The rats scampered off in the direction Ratsputin had fled, leaving me alone, panting, on the stone floor.

I looked up, expecting to see Porthos and the Royal Guards coming to my rescue and instead saw—

Camille rounding the bend of the staircase. She stood at the bottom and grinned at me, waving her paws, casting huge shadows on the walls.

"I know you like to work alone," she quipped. "But I figured you wouldn't mind a little help."

"How did you find me here?"

Camille shrugged. "I followed you."

So much for my MI9 training.

A soft, plaintive meow echoed through the darkness.

I met Camille's eyes silently, and we padded cautiously down the dark tunnel, following the sounds of a rattling iron chain. It was coming from a small alcove with a mud floor. I stepped closer, peering inside.

Hollow eyes stared out from the darkness. A mangy cat caked with mud lay there. A thick iron collar around his neck was attached to the wall by a chain.

"Furrdinand?" I asked.

12

Here We Go Again

BY THE Great Round Food Dish! Your Highness!" a voice said. "I thought I'd never be rescued."

I squinted into the darkness. Underneath all that mud, I felt certain the cat in the iron collar was not a Bengal. In fact, he looked rather like a potato on four toothpicks . . . a Chartreux!

"Papa!" Camille cried.

"Camille, my kitten!" the older cat sobbed. "You're all right!"

"Of course I am, Papa!"

"Ratsputin said he had a vision you were hurt. Attacked by rats. He led me here and—"

My ears twitched. "I hate to break this up," I said, "but I think the rats are returning." Sure enough, the faint squeaking of rats was growing louder and louder. I nodded to Camille. "They must have figured out that we tricked them."

The eyes of the older Chartreux widened in panic, and he tugged in vain at the collar. His neck was missing fur in places. "Go! Camille, I couldn't bear it if anything happened to you. You can't get me out of this collar!"

"On the contrary," I said, flexing a claw.

I was an excellent lockpick, a skill that had proved useful on more than one occasion. After a few moments, I had the collar off.

"Your Highness," the older cat said in awe. "How did you . . . ?"

The rats were almost upon us. Here we go again.

"No time to explain. Run!"

We raced down a dark passage, the sound of rats echoing loudly behind us.

"Do you know a way out of here?" I shouted to Camille.

"Of course," she said, and then gave me a look. "I keep forgetting you don't know. We played in these tunnels as kittens! Follow me!"

She raced ahead, her little legs pumping fast. We followed her through a set of twisty little passages all alike. They curved this way and that with no apparent rhyme or reason. I was completely turned around, but the squeaking of the rats became more and more faint.

"I think we lost them," Camille said in satisfaction, pausing next to a crumbling wall to catch her breath.

"What now?" I panted.

"There's a way out over here," she said, gesturing toward a dark, wet-smelling tunnel.

Soon we found ourselves creeping through a long, low tunnel with channels of running water on either side. The way ahead was bright and opened into the bottom of a deep cistern blanketed with a thick carpet of fallen leaves. A huge tree, several hundred years old, had tumbled down the stones along one side of the cistern and grown all the way up to ground level. High in the sky, a bright moon shone down.

"It's beautiful," I said, looking up where the rim of cistern framed a small circle of sky.

Camille smiled wistfully. "Yes, we—Furrdinand and I—used to come here." She pointed to a hole at the base of the tree. "It's hollow all the way up, and an easy climb."

I moved closer to examine it.

"Now see here, kitten," her father was saying. "What do you mean 'Furrdinand and I'? He's standing right in front of you!"

"Shh!" I hissed in warning. I motioned with my head.

Inside the entrance to the hollow tree were the three genets, fast asleep.

These were night creatures, I remembered, and shouldn't even be sleeping now. They could wake up at any moment.

"Is this the only way out?" I whispered.

Camille nodded and whispered back, "As far as I know. Do you think we can make it back past the rats?"

I made up my mind. "We'll have to chance it." I turned to Camille's father. "You first."

The old Chartreaux crept carefully around the sleeping genets. But luck was not with us. At that moment, a cloud passed in front of the moon, and there was a rumble of thunder.

One of the genets abruptly opened an eye and snarled. The other two's eyes snapped open, and Camille's father froze.

"Hey, sleepyheads!" I called, diverting their attention. "Ready for another beating?"

The genets whirled to face me, and Camille's father took advantage of their distraction to scrabble up the hollow tree to freedom.

"You!" one of them hissed. "When we finish with you this time, you'll—"

Before he'd finished speaking, I sprang at him and sent him tumbling into a fallen stone with a swift kick. He rolled onto the leafy mat, unconscious.

"All meow and no bite." I laughed.

"Get him!" the second genet snarled, still struggling to stand.

But I was already in midair, paws outstretched. I landed, hard, on his belly and knocked the wind out of him. Now I turned to face the third and final genet. We circled each other slowly. He struck a pose, puffed his fur out, and hissed. I couldn't help but snicker. What, did he expect me to growl and spit like a common street brawler?

I feinted to the right, then dashed around to his left. As he whirled to face me, I whipped my tail to the side, tangling it in his feet. He stumbled, and I shoved him hard in the direction of the second genet.

Clonk! Their heads banged together, and they both went out like a light.

"Evolution, three. Missing links, zero," I said, and turned to Camille.

But she was standing stock-still, her eyes wide with fright. Ratsputin stood behind her, an unsheathed claw at her neck. As if for effect, there was a flash of lightning and a crack of thunder.

"Bravo, Furrdinand. But it appears you have lost anyway," he said, grinning that grin of his. "Perhaps we should discuss the terms of your abdication." His claw pricked Camille's neck, and she gasped.

"Let her go," I said in a low voice, advancing slowly through the first fat drops of rain.

Suddenly, the ground went out from under me, and I felt myself falling.

Not again.

13

Drowned Like a Rat

AND THAT is how I came to find myself struggling to stay afloat in rising water up to my chin. Rainwater from all over the castle was rushing in to fill the cistern.

Ratsputin looked down at me and laughed.

"These old castles had excellent drainage," the cat said with a *tsk*ing sound. "I don't know how long you can keep paddling like that, but I do hope you're good at holding your breath." There was another crash of thunder and lightning.

"You'll never get away with this," I said.

"Actually, I will. I'll simply inform the citizens that you died a tragic yet heroic death saving me from the rats."

A rat leaped into view and snickered.

"Personally, I think I'm doing Catlandia a favor by putting a more competent ruler on the throne. Myself," Ratsputin said. "Perhaps the lovely Camille will be my queen?"

"Never, I'd rather die!" I heard her shout.

"Suit yourself," Ratsputin said.

Camille landed with a splash beside me.

"I told you my visions always come to pass. Death by water, as I foresaw," he intoned.

And with that, his head disappeared.

I paddled frantically in the icy water, my head ducking under with every stroke. It wasn't very pleasant, to say the least, but a seasoned counterspy must endure torture on occasion. I recalled how Sir Archibald would lecture his associates on the importance of thinking of something else when faced with such a situation. I found myself thinking of Aaron, and the Greens, and #9 North Tenth Avenue.

Camille was screaming in panic, flailing at the water with claws bared. At this rate, I would lose an eye.

"Camille, calm down!" I said, shouting over the hiss of the rain.

She was breathing too fast. "We're going to drown! We're going to drown!" she kept repeating.

I held my chin up and peered around carefully. If this was a drain, it had to lead out somewhere. Then I saw it! A slightly darker patch below the water level, covered with moss.

"Camille, over here!"

"Help! Help! Help!" Camille was screaming.

I swam over to her and tried to support her, but she lashed out and pushed me under. Finally, I gave up and gave her a good dunking.

"What—what did you do that for," she said, coughing. She was starting to shiver, whether from the cold water or fear, I couldn't tell.

"Look," I said, showing her the outlet. "We can probably swim out that way. Do you think you can make it?"

She shivered. "I'll try."

"Good girl. Now follow me."

I took a deep breath and plunged under the water, clawing away at the moss and opening up the drain. It slanted down, but it was only a short stretch, and I could see light coming from the other end. This was worth the risk. I plunged onward, glancing back to make sure Camille was following. In just a few seconds, we were through and in the stream that served as the castle's moat. I slowed and helped push Camille to the surface. We dragged ourselves to the far bank of the stream and collapsed, panting, on the muddy ground.

Before long, the hard rain eased off to a light sprinkling. It was a typical summer downpour.

When I finally caught my breath, I looked over at Camille. With her wet fur clinging to her body, she looked even more like a potato. A soggy potato.

"What now?" she asked.

I thought for a moment. "Well, Ratsputin thinks we're dead, so he won't send anyone out looking for us. That will buy me some time to find Furrdinand. After all, he's the rightful king of Catlandia. From what I overheard Ratsputin saying, Furrdinand escaped the dungeon not too long ago. We have to assume he's alive, probably in hiding somewhere. But where?"

"I have no idea. I would have found him myself months ago, if I did."

The number one rule of spying is to know your quarry. This means understanding his habits and routines. Sir Archibald always used to say that if you understand how a person thinks, you can catch him. We had once caught a jewel thief at an exclusive shoe store, because Sir Archibald had learned she had a weakness for imported Italian leather shoes.

"What does he like to do?" I asked Camille. "What are his favorite things?"

She thought for a minute. "Well, he likes to eat, more than anything. He's especially partial to bologna."

"Bologna?" I said.

"Yes, American bologna," she said.

"And where can one get it here in France?"

"Occasionally tourists leave it for us here in the garden, but most of the time, I don't know. He always seemed to have a supply on hand whenever he came back from one of his trips."

"That's not much to go on, but I'll check it out."

"I'll go with you," she said, and gave herself a shake. Water flew everywhere.

"No, I need you to catch up with your father. You two should keep a low profile until I come back with Furrdinand, otherwise Ratsputin will come after me. All right? And if you can, find Porthos and explain to him about Furrdinand and me."

"Porthos?" Camille gagged. "But the Royal Guards all—"

"No, he's on our side, Camille. As a matter of fact, he's our best ally at the moment, and I want him to be prepared."

"Got it," she said.

"Now hurry back and get dried off," I added. "You don't want to catch your death of cold, Camille."

Ferme-de-la-Vallée would probably be the closest place to look for American bologna, but it was a long hike, and I wasn't up to it. When I reached the outskirts of Catlandia, I found a country road and used an old trick that I had learned from a cat in America.

I went into the middle of the road and lay down as if injured.

By this time it was early morning, and I didn't need to wait long. Soon, a delivery truck loaded with vegetables came to a screeching stop in front of me.

"*Pauvre chat*," a voice said. "Poor cat." I was gently lifted up and placed in a basket of turnips in the back of the truck.

The truck took me exactly where I'd expected it would—straight into the center of Ferme-de-la-Vallée. When the truck stopped in the marketplace, I hopped out and looked around.

Ferme-de-la-Vallée was a small country town, much like Bois de Perrault, where the Greens were staying. Most of the food stores were clustered around the marketplace, and so I did a little tour of them. There were a sausage shop, a bakery, six cheese shops—no, make that seven—and a small grocery with a sign in the window that read, "We specialize in foods imported from America!"

Bingo.

The door was open, and I strolled right in.

Most of the store was a traditional French épicerie: it carried supplies such as eggs, sugar, and fruit, as well as local wines. Just as I rounded a shelf of pasta, I heard a familiar voice.

"Mommy, look! They have Oreos! I haven't had Oreos in a million years!"

"It's been a week, Lily. And you had a big dessert last night."

"Please please please please please!" she pleaded.

It was the Greens! I ducked back behind the shelf. And then I heard Aaron's voice.

"Dad! Quick! It's Mr. Stink! He's been here all along!"

What was this?

There was a ferocious hiss, and Aaron cried out. "Ow! He scratched me." There was a low, threatening growl.

"I don't think that's Mr. Stink, Aaron," Mr. Green said.

"No, zat is not your cat," the shopkeeper said. "Zis little prince has been coming here for years."

Prince?

"I guess not," Aaron said glumly, and the entire Green family trooped out the front door.

I peeked around the corner to see a large Bengal curled up on a cat bed in the corner, licking a bologna end.

A cat who looked exactly like me.

★ ★ ★

It was a shock to finally come whisker to whisker with my twin. He was a handsome devil.

I strolled up and said, "Prince Furrdinand, I presume."

He blinked as if trying to clear his eyes. "I must be hallucinating from all this bologna," he said. Even his voice sounded like mine. "Are you a vision sent by Ratsputin to torture me?"

"Torture?"

"Like the rats. The rats!" He squeezed his eyes shut. "Those little red eyes in the darkness. Those sharp teeth!"

"Camille sent me," I said, giving a slight bow. "The name is Bristlefur, James Edward Bristlefur."

"But why do you look like me?"

The question hung in the air for a moment.

"Because I'm your twin brother," I said softly.

I watched the emotions twitch through his whiskers. He looked sad and hopeful at the same time.

"My brother?" he whispered finally. "I've always dreamed of having a brother. But Mother said I was the only kitten who survived."

"She hid me away at a young age. It's a long story," I

explained with a sigh. "I'm afraid I have some bad news. Your mother"—and here I hesitated—"*our* mother is dead."

"Dead?"

I nodded.

"Did she suffer at the end?" Furrdinand asked, and I heard the grief in his voice.

"No," I said. "She thought I was you. She told me that she had always loved you."

Furrdinand sniffed. "So I'm king now, then?"

"Yes, and you have to go back to your people," I said.

"But wait. If you're my brother, *you* can be king. They'll never know the difference."

I was puzzled. "Don't you want to go back?"

"Go back, and spend every waking moment looking over my shoulder? Everyone's out to get me. I even got attacked by a pack of genets last week, and I barely escaped."

"I took care of them. And we can take care of Ratsputin."

"It's not about Ratsputin. I never wanted to be king. How could I ever be as good as dear old Dad, savior of Catlandia? The first cat in a thousand years to drive the rats out. Me? I'm afraid of rats."

I sighed. "But what about Camille?"

"They'd never let me marry her anyway. She's not a Bengal."

"Brother," I said in a firm voice, placing my paw on his. "*You* are the king now. You can do whatever you want."

His lips curled into a slow smile. "That's right, I can."

"That's the spirit!"

"Do you have a plan?" he asked.

I grinned. "As a matter of fact, I do."

14

The Return of the King

I CREPT UP the secret stair that led to the tower room. There was a mouse carving on the inside, too, and I pressed it to open the secret panel. I was in.

A platoon of Royal Guards turned a corner, and I melted into the shadows. Handy stuff, the old MI9 training. They were escorting a pair of Abyssinian noblecats, apparently against their will. Athos was at the head of the group, looking a little glassy-eyed.

"I must protest," one of them was saying. "This is most irregular! The lords must be certain that King Furrdinand is truly dead before crowning another king."

"Not to mention, there are rules of succession!" the other Abyssinian added. "I demand the right to investigate this Ratsputin's pedigree! I find it hard to believe that my own claim is any less—"

"Silence!" Athos said. "It is treason to speak against the King!"

"He's not a king until he's crowned with all the lords in attendance," the first cat said haughtily. "And I refuse to go." He sat back on his haunches.

One of the Royal Guards took hold of him by the scruff of the neck and dragged him forward.

"Attendance is mandatory," Athos said.

I followed them from a careful distance to an open courtyard. The space was filled from one end to the other with hundreds of cats. At the far end, lounging on an enormous bed made of old rags, sat Ratsputin. He looked smugly over the assembly in front of him, protected on all sides by the Royal Guards. Porthos stood to one side with a sour expression on his face.

Ratsputin stood and waved a paw for silence.

"Noble and common cats of Catlandia, it touches my heart that you have all come to my coronation," he began.

"He doesn't waste any time, this one," I muttered to myself.

"No, he don't," a voice nearby said.

It was one of the old cats with fleas. "Bit of a rush,

this, if you ask me." He looked at me with cloudy eyes. " 'Ere now, don't you look familiar?"

"Don't think so," I said quickly, and pressed forward.

Ratsputin was still talking. "I stand before you filled with sadness at the loss of your queen and then your king in a span of only two days. But within sorrow, there is also joy. Since the days of the Great Round Food Dish, our kind has always known that there is time and place for everything in this world. We have always known. . . ."

His deep voice droned on and on, and I could feel myself growing sleepy. He was trying to hypnotize the entire crowd!

"Not so fast, Ratboy," I called out in a loud, clear voice, stepping onto a low pile of rubble.

"What?" Ratsputin blurted. "But you're dead!"

"Am I?"

"I killed you myself! How many lives do you *have?*" he moaned.

Everyone in the court gasped.

"What's this?" Porthos demanded. "Guards, arrest Ratsputin at once!"

But the Royal Guards closed ranks, protecting Ratsputin.

Ratsputin grinned at me malevolently. "Guards," he

said, pointing a paw at me. "Arrest that cat!"

Like sharks going after chum, the Royal Guards swiveled to face me.

Porthos leaped in front of them. "Stop! What are you doing? As your captain—" The Royal Guards shouldered him aside, and he ran in front of them again. "As your captain, I order to you to stop."

I backed slowly away from the phalanx of Royal Guards. As one, they began to growl at me, the fur on their backs slowly rising.

"Athos," Porthos was saying, running back and forth in front of the row of guards. "D'Artagnan! What's wrong with you? Halt!" He waved a paw in front of their eyes, but they just kept coming. Porthos was trampled underfoot.

My eyes scanned the crowd. Where was Furrdinand? Had his nerve failed him? My plan wouldn't work without him.

The growling of the guards went down a notch in pitch, and I could see that they were about to attack. I had no choice but to pull my last trick out of my fur.

"*Krisi,*" I shouted.

The Royal Guards stopped in their tracks, expressionless as zombies.

Ratsputin snarled, and I flashed him a cocky grin.

"Guards," I said, "arrest Ratsputin."

The Royal Guards instantly leaped into action, converging on Ratsputin this time, claws bared, fur fluffed.

"*Krisi,*" Ratsputin hissed. Instantly, the Royal Guards went still again. "Throw Furrdinand in the dungeon and pull out his whiskers one by one."

The Royal Guards turned and advanced on me again. Porthos had climbed to his feet and ran to my defense. "Run, your Majesty! I'll hold them off!"

"Stop!" a voice cried from above. Everyone did.

Furrdinand, impeccably groomed, a collar of gold around his neck, sat proudly upon a surviving archway attached to the fallen walls of the chapel.

He looked down his nose at the rabble below. "Firstly, the proper title is *King* Furrdinand. And secondly, that is not Furrdinand." He picked his way down the ruins until he stood beside me, inside the encircling rank of Royal Guards, who looked at one another in dull confusion. In a low voice he continued, "I am King Furrdinand."

Once again, everyone in the court gasped.

"Get him! Get them both!" shrieked Ratsputin.

At this, the Royal Guards leaped at the King and me, bowling over Porthos.

It was time to stop playing this game of cat and mouse.

"Krisi," I shouted. "I release you from your spell. From now on, the only Russian you should care about is Ratsputin."

The Royal Guards blinked and shook their heads.

Porthos took charge. "Guards," he said with a grin of deep satisfaction. "Ratsputin is an enemy of the kingdom. Seize him!"

Before anyone could move a paw, there was a bright flash and cloud of smoke.

Ratsputin was gone.

15

The Order of the Hairball

RATSPUTIN HAD escaped through a hidden trap-door, but his army of rats remained.

With the help of the Royal Guards, Furrdinand and I repeated his father's great feat and drove the rats from the kingdom.

Camille joined us on the rodent hunt. True to her Chartreux breeding, she proved an excellent mouser. Even Porthos was impressed.

"Milady," he said grudgingly. "If Furrdinand chooses you as his queen, well then, I . . . I will be proud to serve you."

"If?" she said, casually cleaning a paw. "You mean 'when,' don't you? But no matter. If Furrdinand decides to keep you as Captain of the Royal Guards, I shall be proud to order you about."

Porthos stood speechless for a moment, until he noticed her eyes twinkling, and they both laughed.

That night, there was a great feast in the courtyard. Camille and her father sat at the King's left paw, and I sat on his right.

"Well, you don't have to worry about your father's legacy now, Your Majesty," I said to Furrdinand as the meal drew to a close. "He would have been proud."

Furrdinand looked at me sadly. "He was your father too, James. I wish you could have known him. He was a great cat."

I sighed.

He batted me on the shoulder. "But we've found each other now, brother. You will stay here with me, won't you? We make a good team. We could rule Catlandia together!"

Camille nodded, and my brother placed his paw on hers. "Family is so important." She looked at her father.

"Well, I—" I began.

Suddenly, Furrdinand got to his feet. "May I have your attention please, everyone," he meowed loudly. And in the resulting hush he coughed, retched, and hacked up a . . . *hairball*?

Appalled, I looked around, but everyone in the court was smiling.

"Kneel," Furrdinand whispered with a wink.

I did.

"I present to you, James Edward Bristlefur, the Order of the Hairball, Catlandia's highest award for gallantry, named in the days of King Artfur. The story

goes that one spring a well-groomed lady of the court was overcome with shedding fur and hacked up a hairball at a state dinner. Rather than allow her to suffer a moment's embarrassment, King Artfur rushed to her side and claimed it as his own. Only once in a generation is this high honor bestowed upon a worthy cat, but, I daresay, more than one generation will pass again before any cat deserves it as much as you, brother."

I didn't know what to say.

"Three cheers for James," Porthos shouted.

Meow meow mreow! Meow meow mreow! Meow meow mreow!

But above the din of cats meowing, a single voice rang through loud and clear.

"He's got to be here somewhere," I heard Aaron say.

My boy!

"Excuse me," I said. I leaped to the ruined wall and looked out.

Aaron and Mr. Green were walking through the early morning light across the ruins with the Cat Tracker. They had rigged it with an extremely long antenna made from coat hangers.

"I'm still not getting a signal," Aaron said. "What if the collar broke?"

Mrs. Green and Lily came into view.

"Do you hear all that meowing?" Mrs. Green asked. "It's like a cat party or something. Is there a full moon?"

"You know, Aaron," Mr. Green said, "we have to get back to Paris. Our flight home is the day after tomorrow."

"We'll find him," Aaron said, twiddling the knobs on the Cat Tracker.

Mr. Green placed a gentle hand on my boy's shoulder. "I'll miss him too, Aaron, but we can get another cat when we get home, if you want."

"No we can't! No one will ever replace Mr. Stink. He's the best cat ever!" Aaron said in an indignant voice.

And that was when I knew that the family I had been looking for had been under my whiskers all along. When it came to choosing between my birthright and my boy, there was no choice. There never had been.

"You're going, aren't you?" a voice asked.

I turned to see Furrdinand sitting next to me.

"Yes," I said. "That's my boy."

"What's he like, your boy?" he asked, curious.

"He's just a boy," I said with a shrug. "But he's my boy."

He bowed his head. "I'll miss you, brother."

"And I'll miss you. If you ever find yourself in New Jersey, look me up. Woodland Park. Parkside Pet Foods."

He nodded.

I started off and then paused, looking back. "Just ask for Mr. Stink."

16

The Lair of the Six-Toed Cat

I T WAS a beautiful summer day, and the wind ruffled my fur as we rode along the French countryside. I sat on my boy's lap in the backseat, content.

"What do you think he was doing all this time?" Mr. Green asked.

"Probably up to no good, knowing this trouble-maker," Mrs. Green said.

Excuse me, I wanted to say. In the last few days I had found my true mother, defeated a villain, restored a king to his rightful throne, and helped drive the rats from Catlandia! *A little respect, please.*

"I can't wait to get home," Aaron said. "I'm sick of France!"

"I thought we were going to go to EuroDisney?" Lily whined.

"We didn't have time because we had to find Mr. Stink," Mrs. Green explained. "Don't you think finding Mr. Stink was more important than going on some ride?"

Lily stuck her tongue out at me. "But I *really* wanted to go to EuroDisney!"

Aaron snorted. "You are so lame, Lily."

"Would you look at that," Mr. Green said. "We're nearly out of gas."

"There's a station up ahead," Mrs. Green said, pointing.

The little car pulled into the petrol station, and Mr. Green got out of the car and began to fill the tank.

"You better go to the bathroom, Lily," Mrs. Green said. "It's a long drive to Paris."

"I don't have to go!"

"Now Lily," her mother said.

"I don't!"

Mrs. Green sighed, getting out of the car. "Fine, Lily, but you better not ask us to pull over."

"Now you stay there, Mr. Stink," Aaron ordered,

and gave me a rough pat on the head. "I'm gonna go get a soda."

"Get me one, too!" Lily said.

I looked out the window at the busy little petrol station. Here and there cars were pulling in, and people were wandering inside to get snacks. But then I saw something that made my hackles rise. A fluffy white cat was stalking Aaron across pavement.

Macavity!

I meowed loudly through a crack in the window to try to get Aaron's attention, but he didn't hear me. Macavity did, though, for he turned around to face me. And that's when I saw the other side of his face.

His face was marred by a wicked-looking set of scars across his cheek and eye. Scars from where I had scratched him in our last encounter. He looked at me angrily and flashed an evil grin, extending a paw with six deadly claws unsheathed.

"What do you want, Mr. Stink?" Lily asked.

I looked wildly around me. I had to get out of this car—now! I suddenly remembered a bit of advice Sir Archibald had given his trainees at MI9 head-quarters: when you're surrounded, try to create a diversion.

I leaped onto the front seat and began pressing on

the horn. It made a loud noise.

"Hey, Mr. Stink! What are you doing?" Lily said.

"Lily, stop that right now!" Mr. Green said from outside.

"Mr. Stink!" Lily shouted. "You're getting me in trouble!" She reached over the seat to grab me, but I easily evaded her. I pressed on the horn again. She squealed, opened her door, and ran around to come at me from the driver's side door.

In a split second, I leaped back over the seat and out the open door, speeding across the ground. I barreled into the six-toed Persian just as he reached out to swipe at Aaron.

Macavity was knocked to the ground.

"What the—?" Aaron asked, turning around. "Hey!"

Leave my family alone! I hissed.

Never! Macavity snarled, and kicked out with his hind legs, knocking me back. I was up in an instant and watched as he dashed into the woods.

"No, Mr. Stink!" Aaron shouted, stomping his foot. "Bad cat!"

But I had no choice. If I didn't take care of the Persian now, permanently, it would never end.

I raced after Macavity.

★ ★ ★

"Catch me if you can, James!" he called over his shoulder as he bounded over fallen tree limbs. For such a fat cat, he could really move.

I followed him along the high bank of a swiftly flowing river, our paws sending pebbles down to the roaring rapids below. He ran up a ridge and across a rotting log that had fallen across the river. I lost him on the other side, but then I heard a scrabbling on the cliff above me. Macavity was making good use of his thumblike extra toe scaling the rocky terrain.

"Give up, Macavity," I called out.

"Give up?" He looked down at me and laughed. "How amusing."

At last, I reached a narrow catwalk at the top. I heard an enormous roar, and saw the source: the river passed through a crack in the cliff and crashed below in an enormous waterfall. The giant spray of mist created a permanent rainbow I might have admired on another occasion.

"Mr. Stink!" I heard a voice call, and peered over to see Aaron standing far below. He had a panicked look on his face. "Stay right there! I'll get help!"

Quite resourceful, my boy, I thought. One day, I'd have to make up for all the trouble I'd caused him lately.

"You were always such a fool, James," Macavity's voice purred.

I whirled. The six-toed Persian slithered out of the shadows. Behind him, I could see several empty bags of cat food tucked into a small cave. Stolen from the Le Chat Gourmet factory, no doubt. I had found Macavity's lair.

"A fool?" I mocked. "Would a fool have tracked you back to your hideout?"

"I *let* you find me! What do you think?"

I snickered. "The same way you *let* me leave that scar on your cheek? So much for your dreams of being a showcat! I don't think Le Chat Gourmet will come calling any time soon."

He snarled and came at me, and we tumbled to the ground. I caught him on the nose with one claw, and he yelped.

"You'll pay for that!" he screamed. "You'll pay for everything you've done to me."

"Not in this life," I shot back. "Not in a hundred lives."

"But James," he said. "You only have *nine* lives. And I think they've run out."

In an instant, he flung himself at me and we went over the cliff together.

"Noooo!" I heard Aaron shout.

We soared through the air in a tangle of fur and claws. Macavity snarled and sank his fangs into my back. The roar of the approaching waterfall filled my ears, and I couldn't help but wonder if I should have seen this coming.

Oh bother was my last thought before we vanished into the mist.

THE TAIL ENDS HERE FOR NOW!
(OR DOES IT??)

Authors' Addendum

THIS COMPLETES our translation work on the bulk of the shortpaw notes James Edward Bristlefur left behind in his safe house before his disappearance. As you have read, the events of the narrative have thrown into question the whole authorship of his notes. If Mr. Stink survived his fall, why do his notes end here? If not, how could he have left anything afterward for us to find? One startling possibility is that Mr. Stink is not the author of the documents we discovered.

A tantalizing alternative remains. There were quite a large number of unrelated fragments that we were unable to find a place for in the narrative. We cannot be certain whether these are random recollections of Bristlefur's earlier adventures with Sir Archibald or whether "Mr. Stink" miraculously survived his fall somehow and found his way back to America. Only time—and further study—will tell.

So that we do not cause the general public undue concern, it is our recommendation that The Stink Files be sealed until we are able to resolve this enigma.

Respectfully submitted,
Holm & Hamel
Special to MI9

Attention All Agents:
Have you seen Mr. Stink in your neighborhood? Please e-mail photos of cats you think might be Mr. Stink to sighting@stinkfiles.com.